Around the Neighborhood
A Counting Lullaby

adapted by **Sarah L. Thomson**   illustrated by **Jana Christy**

Amazon Children's Publishing

Amazon Publishing
Attn: Amazon Children's Books
P.O. Box 400818
Las Vegas, NV 89149
www.amazon.com/amazonchildrenspublishing

The illustrations are rendered digitally.
Book design by Vera Soki
Editor: Robin Benjamin

Printed in China (W)
First edition
10 9 8 7 6 5 4 3 2 1

Library of Congress Cataloging-in-Publication Data
Thomson, Sarah L.
Around the neighborhood : a counting lullaby / adapted by Sarah L.
Thomson ; illustrated by Jana Christy. — 1st ed.
p. cm.
Summary: This adaptation of the old nursery poem "Over in the
Meadow" introduces neighborhood animals and their young and
the numbers one through ten.
ISBN 978-0-7614-6164-7 (hardcover) —
ISBN 978-0-7614-6165-4 (ebook)
1. Nursery rhymes. 2. Children's poetry. [1. Nursery rhymes. 2.
Animals—Poetry. 3. Neighborhoods—Poetry. 4. Counting.] I.
Christy, Jana, ill. II. Title.
PZ8.3.T3274Ar 2012   398.8'4—dc23   2011034872

For Deva, my one and only
—S.L.T.

To my mom and dad
—J.C.

Around the neighborhood,
inside a room full of sun,
lived a happy, laughing mother
and her little baby one.

"Play," said the mother.
"I play," said the one.
So they played and were glad
in the room full of sun.

Around the neighborhood,
beside a house painted blue,
lived an old father hound dog
and his little puppies two.

"Sniff," said the father.
"We sniff," said the two.
So they sniffed and were glad
by the house painted blue.

Around the neighborhood,
beneath the shade of a tree,
lived an old mother calico
and little kittens three.

"Pounce," said the mother.
"We pounce," said the three.
So they pounced and were glad
in the shade of the tree.

Around the neighborhood,
upon a web near a door,
lived an old father spider
and his spiderlings four.

"Spin," said the father.
"We spin," said the four.
So they spun and were glad
on the web near a door.

Around the neighborhood,
between a swing and a slide,
lived an old mother ladybug
and little beetles five.

"Crawl," said the mother.
"We crawl," said the five.
So they crawled and were glad
by the swing and the slide.

Around the neighborhood,
beside a wall made of bricks,
lived an old father rabbit
and his little bunnies six.

"Hop," said the father.
"We hop," said the six.
So they hopped and were glad
by the wall made of bricks.

Around the neighborhood,
where wildflowers grow free,
lived an old mother queen bee
and her seven honeybees.

"Hum," said the mother.
"We hum," said the bees.
So they hummed and were glad
where the flowers grow free.

Around the neighborhood,
atop a tall iron gate,
lived an old father black crow
and his little hatchlings eight.

"Caw," said the father.
"We caw," said the eight.
So they cawed and were glad
on the tall iron gate.

Around the neighborhood,
by where a stream bends and winds,
lived an old mother mallard
and her little ducklings nine.

"Dive," said the mother.
"We dive," said the nine.
So they dove and were glad
where the stream bends and winds.

Around the neighborhood,
the day had come to an end
for an old father swallow
and his little swallows ten.

"Soar," said the father.
"We soar," said the ten.
So they soared and were glad
as day came to an end.

Around the neighborhood,
when all the playing was done,
lived a tired, smiling mother
and her little baby one.

"Sleep," said the mother.
"I sleep," said the one.
So they slept and were glad
when the playing was done.

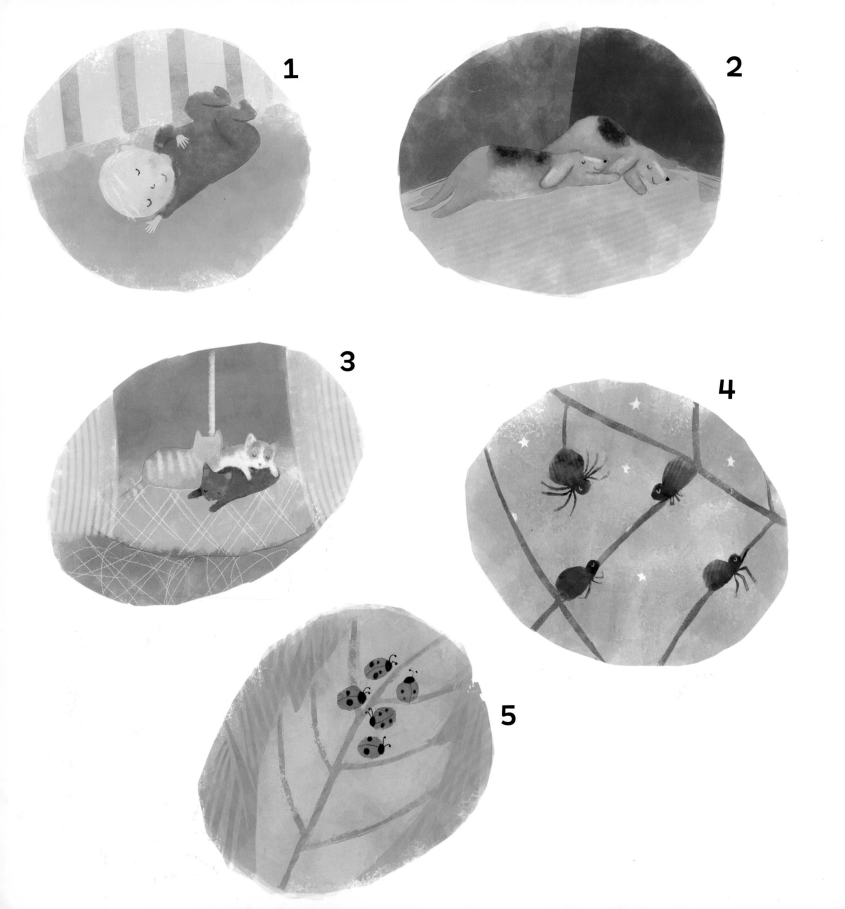

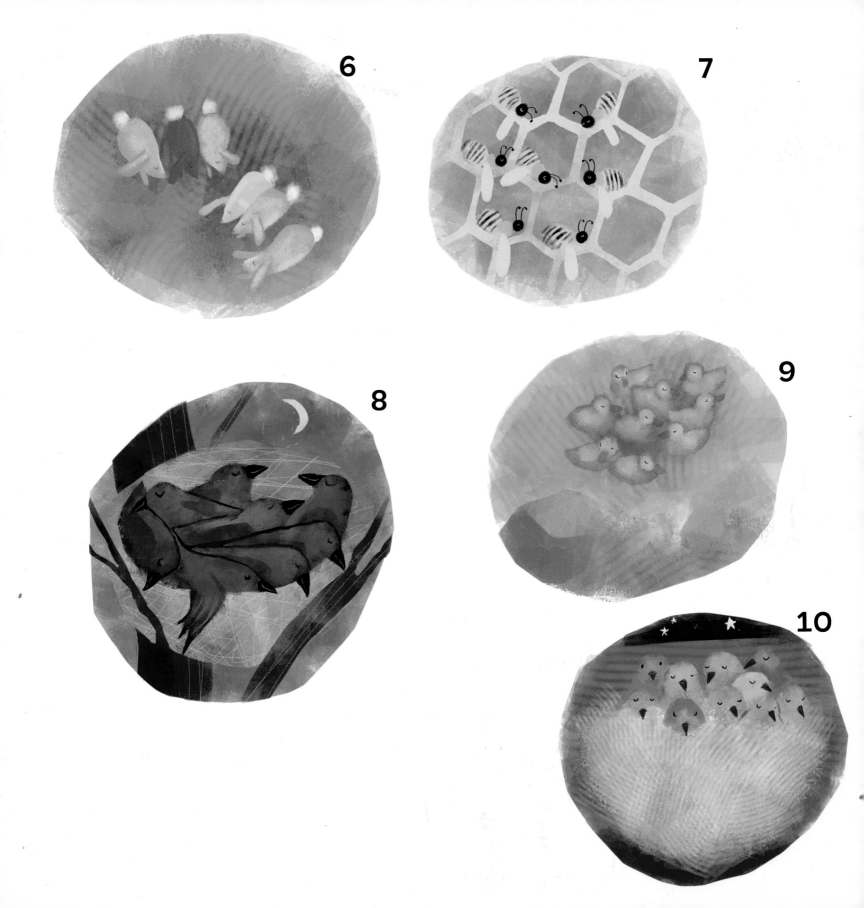

Author's Note

Around the Neighborhood is based on an old folk song from the southern Appalachians. The song is often known as "Over in the Meadow," but sometimes has other titles. Cecil Sharp, a folk-song collector, included it in a 1917 collection of tunes under the name "'Sing,' Said the Mother." Sometimes the song is attributed to Olive A. Wadsworth, the pen name of author Katharine Floyd Dana. She did include a version (hers counted up to twelve) in her novel *Kit, Fan, Tot, and the Rest of Them,* published in 1870. It's "a funny little song" that Tot's mother uses to teach her how to count. The wording suggests that Dana did not invent the song but simply included a folk song she knew, imagining it was the kind of thing a mother might sing to a young child.

In the end, it's hard to say where folk songs really come from. They move from person to person, changing as they go. If the tune or the words or the mood stays in our heads, the song survives. There are many versions of "Over in the Meadow" known today. The one thing that stays the same in all of them is a warm, loving, teaching relationship between a parent and a child. I often sang the song to my young daughter. We liked the version John Langstaff created for his picture book *Over in the Meadow,* first published in 1957. But my little girl didn't encounter many of the animals in the song (foxes, beavers, bullfrogs) on our walks around the neighborhood. However, there were animals she was always excited to see—crows, ladybugs, cats, dogs. I wanted to make a version of the song for her that would include the animals that she loved and saw daily.

By the time this book is published, my girl will be a bit too old to be sung to sleep. But still, sweetheart—this is for you.   —S.L.T.